THE Nutcracker

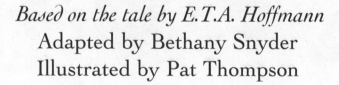

Based on the tale by E.T.A. Hoffmann
Adapted by Bethany Snyder
Illustrated by Pat Thompson

Dalmatian Press

Christmas Eve! No other evening is *so* exciting (as I'm sure you'll agree). Marie, who was seven years old, was eagerly awaiting the magic of Christmas Eve. She and her older brother Fritz had been listening to the comings and goings and strange noises from the living room all day. Fritz had even spied a dark, hunched man coming from the living room. This could only be their godfather, Papa Drosselmeier.

At last, after a whole day of listening and waiting and nearly bursting with excitement, Marie and her brother were allowed into the living room. And what do you think they saw when they came through the door? Why, just the most beautiful, shining Christmas tree that ever was.

Little candles twinkled on the branches—and there were little toys, and candies, and ornaments, too!

"Oh, how marvelous!" Marie exclaimed.

Fritz jumped up in the air and hollered,

"Stupendous!"

And what was over here? A wooden horse for Fritz (who simply adored horses) and a whole new set of soldiers for his army. For Marie there was a new doll (Marie immediately named her Clara, because no doll should have to go very long without a proper name), and the most beautiful dress in all the world, with colored ribbons and buttons.

And then Papa Drosselmeier came into the room with a splendid surprise—a wonderful castle with golden towers and sparkling windows! And there was a tiny Papa Drosselmeier, no taller than your finger, which appeared at the castle door—going out and going in again.

The grownups *oohed* and *ahhed* over the castle. Marie, who was a polite little girl, thanked her godfather for the castle before going to play with her new doll.

Marie was just bending over to pick up Clara when
she spied a little man hiding under the lowest branches
of the tree. "Father, whom does that little man belong to?"
Marie asked.

"He is Nutcracker, and he belongs to everyone.
Let me show you what he can do."

Father picked up the odd-looking man. He
put an almond between the little man's teeth,
pulled down on Nutcracker's short wooden cape,
and—*Crack!*—pieces of shell fell away and
Father handed the nut to Marie.

"Wonderful!" she said. "He is an adorable
little man."

"Well," said Father, "since you love him
so dearly already, I will place him in your keeping.
Of course, you must share him with Fritz."

"Oh, I will!" said Marie, as she hugged the
strange wooden man.

Marie put only the softest and smallest nuts in
Nutcracker's mouth. She did not want
to ruin his big smile or his wide, white teeth.

"Let me see!" a voice demanded.

Marie turned to see Fritz, who grabbed Nutcracker from his sister's hands. He started feeding Nutcracker the very hardest nuts! Nutcracker's teeth gave in with a terrible crunch and three teeth popped out onto the floor.

Poor Nutcracker! He looked so fine in his uniform and shiny black boots— but he had a broken jaw.

"You give him back!" Marie said. She took Nutcracker in her arms. "You are a terrible monster, Fritz."

"I don't know why you would like such an ugly old thing anyway," said Fritz.

"Well, I do!" Marie cried. "I'm going to take care of him and make him better."

She bandaged his broken jaw with a ribbon of silk from her new dress. Then she took her wounded Nutcracker to the large glass cabinet in the living room, where they kept their favorite dolls and toys.

Marie looked at Clara. "I'm sorry, Clara," she said, "but Nutcracker is badly wounded, and I know you won't mind giving up your bed to him, now will you?" (Clara did not mind.) "Very good. Now, rest well, Nutcracker. It is late. Papa Drosselmeier will fix your teeth and jaw tomorrow and you'll be good as new."

As Marie turned to go upstairs to bed, the tall grandfather clock chimed the midnight hour. Then the strangest thing happened. Marie heard strange squeakings and clatterings behind her. She spun around, and—could it be? Hundreds of mice were pouring out from under the sofa and chairs, and from between the cracks in the doors!

Then a terrible rumbling shook the floor, and up came a giant Mouse King with seven heads! And on those heads were seven gold crowns!

"I've come for Nutcracker and he will be mine!" he shouted.

Nutcracker leaped from the glass cabinet, leading Fritz's toy soldiers! The army fought bravely—shooting gumdrop cannonballs at the awful mice.

But the Mouse King
suddenly sprang at
Nutcracker!

"Stay away from him!"
Marie shouted.

She threw her left shoe
into the fray—and it hit the Mouse King right on his many heads. He ran
away with all the other mice. Well, Marie fainted right then and there.

Marie awoke in her very own bed. Had it all been a dream? She looked up and saw Papa Drosselmeier smiling gently at her.

"I have something for you, my dear…"

And do you know what it was? Why, it was Nutcracker! And he was mended! His teeth were in straight and his jaw worked perfectly. Marie hugged him tightly She had tears in her eyes as she thanked her dear Papa Drosselmeier.

That night, Marie couldn't sleep. Just after the clock chimed midnight, she heard strange sounds—clanging and crashing from the living room!—then a terrible squeak!—then a knock on the bedroom door!—and then a voice crying:

"Marie! Open the door. I have wonderful news!"

Marie recognized the voice of Nutcracker and let him in.

"I have defeated the Mouse King!" Nutcracker exclaimed. "It was you who gave me the courage to defeat that nasty creature. To thank you, I wish to give you these."

He handed her seven tiny gold crowns. Marie clasped her hands with delight.

"I must tell you, dear Marie, that I am really a king," said Nutcracker. "A king of the most wondrous land in all the world! Toyland! And now, will you join me as I travel to my kingdom to celebrate this happy occasion?"

Marie could think of nothing she would rather do.

Marie followed Nutcracker to the front closet, where he revealed a hidden ladder. Marie was *just* small enough to climb up this ladder, and soon found herself standing in a sweet-smelling meadow.

"This is Candy Meadow," said Nutcracker. "Now we will travel through all of Toyland on our way to Marzipan Castle in the City of Sweets. That is where I live."

Oh, and Toyland was marvelous! They passed through Almond and Raisin Gateway. They watched a charming ballet.

They went by Orange Brook and River Lemonade, and past
Gingerbread City on the Honey River. In each of these places Marie
saw the most amazing things: houses and whole villages made out of
all manner of sweets, and the friendliest people you could ever hope
to meet. There were creatures of all kinds, and they were dancing and
laughing about in the merriest way.

They finally came to a rose-colored lake. Nutcracker summoned a jeweled gondola pulled by dolphins to take them across the water.

On and on, under a moonlit sky, they glided over the lake. There ahead lay the City of Sweets and Marzipan Castle! When they arrived, what do you think Marie saw? Only the most beautiful houses, all made of brightly-colored candies, and a marketplace full of delicious sweets that made her mouth water.

Nutcracker took Marie up to his castle, where she met all the ladies of the house, and the royal pages and such. Everyone was so nice that Marie decided she would *never* leave.

They had a wonderful meal of hundreds of candies and desserts. And then Marie started to yawn and rub her eyes. Can you blame her? She had been through quite a bit of excitement, to say the least (and she had probably eaten a bit too much candy). Indeed, Marie *did* fall fast asleep to the sound of her beloved Nutcracker talking. . .

. . .and when she awoke, she was in her own bed.

"Oh, it just couldn't have been a dream!" she said sadly.

But what was this in her hand? Why, the seven tiny gold crowns that Nutcracker had given her.

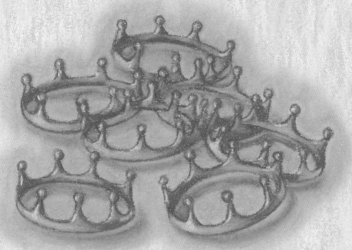

Many, many years later, Marie sat in the living room, gazing at her old, beloved Nutcracker in the glass cabinet.

"Oh, Nutcracker," she said, "if only you were really alive. I would love you just as you are! I don't think you are ugly. I think you are handsome."

Just then Marie's mother came in. "Sit up like a proper young lady," she said. "Papa Drosselmeier's nephew is here to meet you."

"Who?" said Marie, sitting up very straight indeed.

In came a handsome young man.
He smiled, walked over, and took
Marie's hand in his own.

"Oh, sweet Marie,"
he said, "I *am* really alive!
You were kind and gentle
enough to say that you
would love me just as I am. . .
and so, here I am. Now,
would you do me the honor
of becoming my wife—and
queen of all Toyland?"

"Nutcracker—is it really
you?" whispered Marie.
"Of course I will!"

Ah, dear children, who can say how such things

happen in this world—and in the world of toys and dreams?

Who can say how love creates its own magic? And who can

say whether Queen Marie and her beloved King Nutcracker

rule over Toyland to this very day? If you have the eyes

and heart for it, dear children, perhaps someday you

will visit Toyland—and then. . .

you can say.